Angela Kincaid courtesy of Bernard Thornton Artists, London.
ISBN 1 85854 586 2
© Brimax Books Ltd 1997. All rights reserved.
Published by Brimax Books Ltd, Newmarket, England, CB8 7AU, 1997.
Printed in China.

Read to Me Again

By Gill Davies

Illustrated by Angela Kincaid

Brimax · Newmarket · England

Lucy Loppy has a Cold

Lucy Loppy wakes up in the middle of the night. Her nose tickles.

"Atishoo! Atishoo!" she sneezes.

It is a very big sneeze.

"Do not sneeze near me," says Gump Gorilla. He dives back under the covers.

"Do not sneeze near me!" shouts Funky Frog. He pulls his blanket over his head.

"Use your handkerchief," says Elgar Elephant. He ties a knot in his trunk so he doesn't catch any germs.

"I am sorry," says Lucy Loppy.
Then before she can stop herself, she
sneezes again.

"AAATISHOO!" It is a very loud
sneeze.

"I am trying to sleep," says Gump
Gorilla. He takes his quilt and pillow
into another bedroom.

"So am I," says Funky Frog. He follows
Gump Gorilla.

"Can't you be quiet?" says Elgar
Elephant. He follows his friends.

Lucy Loppy begins to cry.

"I cannot help sneezing," she says.

She climbs out of bed and goes into Rosie Ragdoll's bedroom.

"I do not feel well," cries Lucy.

"And everyone is angry with me for sneezing."

Lucy sneezes a very long sneeze.

"Atishooo!" she says.

"You have a bad cold," says Rosie.

"You must stay in bed tomorrow."

"Can I stay in bed too?" asks Funky Frog coming into Rosie's room.

"And me?" asks Gump Gorilla.

"And me?" asks Elgar Elephant.

"No," says Rosie. "You must go to school in the morning."

Rosie goes downstairs to make Lucy a hot drink that will make her feel better.

In the morning, the toys go into the bathroom.

"It's not fair," says Funky Frog as he washes his face.

"I wish I could stay in bed all day," says Elgar Elephant as he pulls on his socks.

"Lucy's only pretending to be ill," says Gump Gorilla as he brushes his hair.

"No I am not!" shouts Lucy.

Then she snuggles back into bed as the other toys go downstairs for breakfast.

Then Funky Frog sneezes as he eats his cereal. It is a very big sneeze. He spills his milk. Gump Gorilla sneezes as he eats his toast. It is a very loud sneeze. Gump drops his toast. Elgar Elephant sneezes as he pours his juice. It is a very long sneeze. The cereal box topples over. Then they all sneeze together.

19

"My throat is sore," says Funky Frog.
"I cannot croak properly."
"My chest hurts. I cannot thump it
anymore," says Gump Gorilla.
"My head aches... And my tusks...
And my ears," groans Elgar Elephant.
He wraps his trunk around his head.
"Oh dear," says Rosie. "I think you
should all go back to bed."

"What is the matter?" asks Lucy Loppy as the toys come back into the bedroom.

"I am sorry we were angry with you," whispers Funky.

"You were right," says Gump. "This cold is horrible."

"Atishoo! I'm cold and shivery!" says Elgar Elephant.

So all the toys have to spend the day in bed!

The next morning, Funky Frog wakes up first.

"I can croak again!" he says.

"I can thump my chest without it hurting!" says Gump Gorilla.

"I am not sneezing anymore," says Elgar Elephant.

"Good!" says Lucy Loppy. She laughs as her friends all try to hug her at once.

25

Can you spot five differences between these two pictures?

What are they doing?

sneezing

washing

brushing

sleeping

Gump Gorilla's Squeaky Shoes

Gump Gorilla has a new pair of shoes. They are white and green with stripy laces. He tries them on with his bright red t-shirt and looks in the mirror.
"Are you coming out to play?" asks Lucy Loppy.
"I'll be out in a minute," says Gump.

31

The toys decide to play a game of hide and seek. Lucy Loppy hides under the slide. Funky Frog hides in the bushes. Elgar Elephant hides behind a tree, but his trunk still shows! At last they are all ready. "Ready and coming!" shouts Gump Gorilla and he sets off to find his friends.

33

As soon as Gump begins to walk,
his shoes begin to squeak.
Squeak! Squeak! Squeak!
Gump walks along the path.
Squeak! Squeak! Squeak!
Gump walks over the grass.
The toys can hear Gump coming.
As soon as he gets near, they slip
away and hide somewhere else.
"That's not fair!" he says.

"You should wear your old shoes," says Elgar Elephant. "Then we won't be able to hear you coming."

"No," says Gump. "I do not want to wear my old shoes. I like my new shoes. I will wear them all day. I do not care if they squeak."

"It is your turn to hide now," says Funky Frog to Gump. "Off you go."

The toys hide again.
Elgar Elephant hides in the shed.
Lucy Loppy hides behind a flowerpot.
Gump Gorilla crouches down behind
the sacks of old leaves.
"Ready and coming!" calls Funky Frog,
setting off along the path.
Lucy, Elgar and Gump stay as quiet
and still as they can.

39

Gump tries to move into a more comfortable position. His knees are bent and there is a rose bush scratching his neck. But as soon as Gump moves, his shoes squeak. Now Funky Frog knows exactly where Gump is hiding.

"Found you!" says Funky Frog jumping onto Gump. Gump is angry.

"It's not fair!" he says.

"Go and change your shoes then," says Funky.

"No," says Gump. "I do not want to wear any other shoes. I like my new shoes. I shall wear them all day. I do not care how much they squeak."

The toys go back indoors.

Gump Gorilla walks across the grass.

Squeak! Squeak! Squeak!

He walks along the path.

Squeak! Squeak! Squeak!

He jumps down the garden steps.

Squeak! Squeak! Squeak!

Gump opens the door and goes inside.

Squeak! Squeak! Squeak!

Gump's shoes squeak all the way.

Gump Gorilla sits down and takes off his new shoes. He hugs them against his bright red t-shirt.

"I do not care if you squeak," he says. "You are the best shoes I have ever had!"

Can you spot five differences between these two pictures?

Where are they hiding?

behind a tree

under the slide

in the bushes

behind a sack

Elgar Elephant and the Party

Like all elephants, Elgar the Elephant is BIG! He has big ears and big feet, and a long trunk. Elgar likes eating all the time. He eats as many cakes as he can, and he loves chocolate ice cream. But because Elgar likes to eat so much, all of his clothes are now too small. What could he wear to Rosie Rag's surprise birthday party?

Elgar listens to his friends talking about what they will wear to the party.

"I will wear my red waistcoat and my pink bow-tie," says Funky Frog taking them out of the drawer.

"I will wear my stripy, yellow t-shirt and my new shoes," says Gump Gorilla pulling them out from under the bed.

"I will wear my long, purple dress," says Lucy Loppy holding it up in front of the mirror.

Tears roll down Elgar's face.

"What is the matter, Elgar?" asks Lucy Loppy.

"I have nothing special to wear to the party," says Elgar.

"What about your green dungarees?" asks Lucy.

"They are too small now," says Elgar. He tries on the dungarees, but he cannot do up the buttons.

Elgar follows Gump Gorilla sadly downstairs.

"What is the matter, Elgar?" asks Gump when he sees Elgar's sad face.

"I have nothing special to wear to the party," says Elgar.

"You can borrow my astronaut outfit if you like," says Gump.

He takes it out of the chest in the hall.

Elgar tries to squeeze himself
into the outfit, but it does not fit.
"Oh dear!" he sighs and he sits down
on the stairs.
Funky Frog hops past Elgar. He goes
outside to show the frogs by the pond
his waistcoat and bow-tie.

"What is wrong, Elgar?" asks Funky as Elgar marches outside and stamps up the path into the wood.

"I do not have any nice clothes for the party," says Elgar.

"You can borrow my bow-tie if you like," says Funky.

Funky gives Elgar the bow-tie, but it is far too small, and will not even tie around his trunk.

"I do not think I will go to the party," says Elgar. "I am the only one who has nothing special to wear."

"Cheer up," says Funky. "You look lovely as you are."

Suddenly Gump Gorilla hurries towards them.

"Hurry up," calls Gump. "The party is about to start and we need Elgar to blow up the balloons."

Back indoors, Lucy Loppy is waiting for them.

"Here you are at last!" she says.

"Rosie will arrive at any moment and none of the balloons are ready."

Elgar sucks air into his trunk and after a few puffs he has blown up a roomful of balloons.

The toys cannot find enough places for all the balloons to hang, so they tie some to Elgar. They tie balloons around his legs, tail, ears and trunk. Soon Elgar is covered in balloons. When Rosie Rags arrives she is very surprised to see them all.

"How wonderful!" she cries. "And look at Elgar! What a clever party outfit you are wearing!"

Elgar is so happy he laughs and dances all afternoon.

Can you spot five differences between these two pictures?

What are they wearing?

bow-tie

dress

t-shirt

balloons

Funky Frog's Picnic

Funky Frog is bored. All the toys are busy and he can find nothing to do.

"Will you play with me?" Funky asks Elgar Elephant.

"No," says Elgar. "I am tidying my books."

"Will you play with me?" Funky asks Lucy Loppy.

"No," says Lucy Loppy. "I am painting a picture."

"Will you play with me?" Funky asks Gump Gorilla.

"No," says Gump. "I am cleaning my new shoes."

"It is a lovely sunny morning," says Rosie Rags to Funky. "Why don't you go for a walk? You could take a picnic."

Funky Frog likes peanut butter sandwiches. He makes lots and lots and packs them into his rucksack. Then he sets off down the lane. Soon the thought of the sandwiches in his rucksack makes Funky feel hungry.

"It is only ten o'clock," says Funky. "I cannot eat my picnic yet."

Funky sits down by the stream and watches some toads splashing in the waterfall.

"Come and join us," they call to him. So Funky takes off his rucksack and jumps into the water. He has so much fun swimming and splashing in the water, he forgets how hungry he is.

At last Funky climbs out of the water.

Funky Frog says goodbye to the toads and puts on his rucksack again. Then he sets off along the path.

"Swimming always makes me feel hungry," says Funky. "But it is only eleven o'clock. I cannot eat my picnic yet."

So Funky decides to climb a tree.

He watches some squirrels chasing through the branches.

"Come and join us," call the squirrels.

Funky has lots of fun swinging through the branches and bouncing into soft piles of leaves. He forgets how hungry he feels. When he is tired of swinging through the trees, Funky says goodbye to the squirrels. He collects his rucksack and sets off again along the path.

"Chasing games always make me hungry," says Funky. "But it is twelve o'clock now, so I can eat my picnic."

Funky stops and looks about him.
"The woods are very thick and dark
here," he says. "I think I will try to
find a sunnier place to eat my picnic."
Funky walks down another path. Then
he stops and looks about.
"The path is very hard and stony here,
and there might be foxes. I think I will
try and find a softer, safer place to
eat my picnic." On he walks down
another path.

Funky looks over his shoulder.
He shivers.
"The wood is very cold here,"
he says. "There might be wolves!
I will try and find a warmer, safer
place."
The path gets narrower as Funky
walks along.
"Ooo-er!" says Funky. "I think
I am lost."
Funky begins to cry. He has forgotten
about his picnic. He does not feel
hungry at all.

Suddenly Funky hears voices.

"This way!" calls one voice.

"Follow me!" says another voice.

"He's over here!" says a third voice.

Then all at once Lucy Loppy, Gump Gorilla, Rosie Rags and Elgar Elephant burst through the trees.

"Am I pleased to see you!" says Funky. "How did you know where I was?"

"There is a hole in your rucksack. Your sandwiches have been dropping out all along the path. We followed them!" says Lucy Loppy.

"We have brought a picnic too," says Elgar Elephant.

Then Elgar gives Funky a ride along the path to the sunniest, softest, warmest, safest part of the wood.

The toys eat their picnic of sandwiches, chocolate cake, apples and oranges.

"Getting lost has made me very, very hungry!" says Funky Frog.

Can you spot five differences between these two pictures?

What can you see in the story?

toad

squirrel

fox

waterfall